ALC

Alcott, Louisa May
Kate's Choice

DATE DUE

PRINTED IN U.S.A.

if card is lost from pocket

In Loving Memory of

Elizabeth Kridner

**This Book is placed in the Memorial Section of
The Dominy Memorial Library by**

Wayne Kridner

Presented To:

_____

From:

_____

Date:

_____

Kate's Choice

What Love Can Do

Gwen's Adventure in the Snow

Three Fire-side Stories to
Warm the Heart
by

Louisa May Alcott

Edited by Stephen W. Hines
Illustrations by C. Michael Dudash

BOOKSPAN LARGE PRINT EDITION

RIVER
OAK
PUBLISHING

Tulsa, Oklahoma

This Large Print Edition, prepared especially for Bookspan, contains the complete, unabridged text of the original Publisher's Edition.

Kate's Choice
What Love Can Do
Gwen's Adventure in the Snow

ISBN 0-7394-2000-3

Published by RiverOak Publishing
P.O. Box 700143
Tulsa, Oklahoma 74170-0143

Book design by Koechel Peterson & Associates
Illustrations by C. Michael Dudash

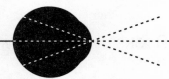

This Large Print Book carries the
Seal of Approval of N.A.V.H.

TABLE OF CONTENTS

Louisa May Alcott was at the height of her literary powers and popularity when she wrote the heartwarming collection of stories you are about to read. Just a few short years earlier, the publication of her beloved classic *Little Women* had made her famous. What years they were!

For a brief period, she was the sole editor of *Merry's Museum,* a magazine for girls. For her salary, a not unprincely sum of five hundred dollars a year, she did much of the writing for the magazine as well as the editing. But she also kept up a steady stream of submissions to other publications, and she was accepted almost every time.

Her output of work was amazing. Louisa May Alcott could work from seven in the morning until late in the evening when inspiration was on her, as it often was during this time. It was from this period of great productivity and success that the stories "Kate's Choice," "What Love Can Do" (originally titled "How It All Happened"), and "Gwen's Adventure in the Snow" (originally titled "How They All Camped Out") came to be written.

BOOK ❧ ONE

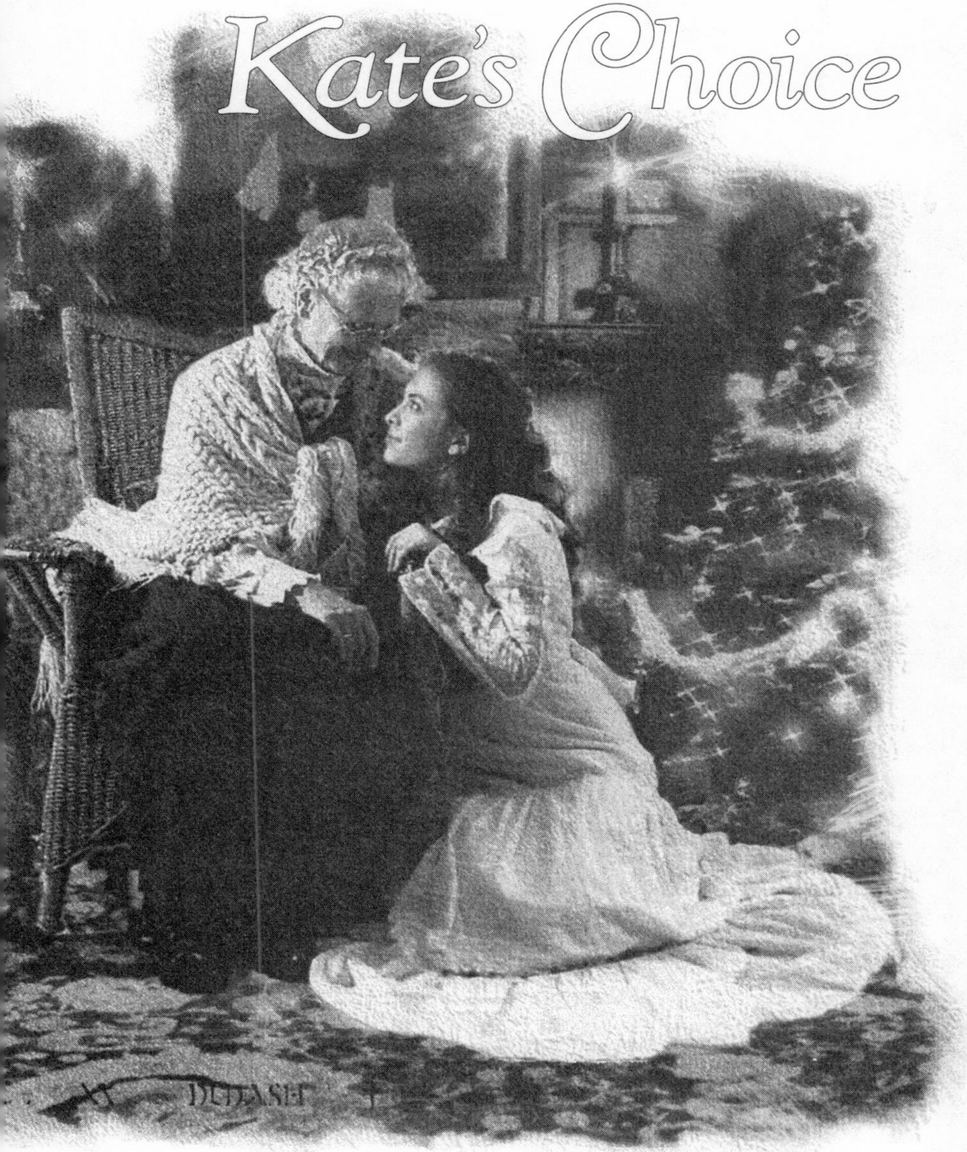
Kate's Choice

Getting Acquainted

"Well, what do you think of her?"

"I think she's a perfect dear and not a bit stuck up with all her money."

"A real little lady and ever so pretty."

"She kissed me lots, and she doesn't tell me to run away, so I love her."

The group of brothers and sisters standing round the fire laughed as little May finished the chorus of praise with these crowning virtues.

Tall Kent had asked the question and seemed satisfied with the general approval of the new cousin who had just arrived from England to live with them.

They had often heard of Kate and rather prided themselves on the fact that she lived in a fine house, was very rich, and sent them charming presents. Now pity was added to the pride, for Kate was an orphan, and all her money could not buy back the parents she had lost.

They had watched impatiently for her arrival, had welcomed her cordially, and after a day spent in trying to make her feel at home, they were comparing notes in the twilight, while Kate was having a quiet talk with Mamma.

"I hope she will choose to live with us. You know she can go to any of the uncles she likes best," said Kent.

"We are nearer her age than any of the other cousins, and Papa is the oldest uncle, so I guess she will," added Milly, the fourteen-year-old daughter of the house.

"She said she liked America," said quiet Frank.

"Wonder if she will give us a lot of her money?" put in practical Fred, who was always in debt.

"Stop that!" commanded Kent. "Mind now, if you ever ask her for a penny, I'll shake you out of your jacket."

"Hush! She's coming," cried Milly, and a dead silence followed the lively chatter.

A fresh-faced, bright-eyed girl of fifteen came in quietly, glanced at the group on the rug, and paused as if uncertain whether she was wanted.

"Come on!" said Fred, encouragingly.

"Would I be in the way?" she asked.

"Oh, dear, no! We were only talking," answered Milly, drawing her cousin nearer with an arm about her waist.

"It sounded like something pleasant," said Kate, not exactly knowing what to say.

"We were talking about you," began Little May. A poke from Frank made her stop to ask, "What's that for? We *were* talking about Kate, and we all said we liked her, so it's no matter if I tell."

"You are very kind," said Kate looking so pleased that the children forgave May's awkward frankness.

"Yes, and we hoped you'd like us and stay with us," added Kent, in the lofty and polite manner that he thought became a young man of his stature.

"I am going to live with all the uncles in turn, and then decide," Kate answered. "Papa wished it." The words made her lips tremble slightly, for her father was the only parent she could remember and had been unusually dear to her for that reason.

⚮ ⚮ ⚮ ⚮ ⚮ ⚮ ⚮ ⚮ ⚮ ⚮ ⚮ ⚮ ⚮ ⚮ ⚮ ⚮ ⚮ ⚮

"Can you play billiards?" asked Fred, who had a horror of seeing girls cry.

"Yes, and I will be glad to teach you."

"You had a pony carriage at your house, didn't you?" added Frank, eager to hear more.

"At Grandma's—I had no other home, you know," answered Kate.

"What will you buy first with your money?" asked May, who seemed determined to ask improper questions.

"I'd buy a grandma if I could," and Kate both smiled and sighed.

"How funny!" said May. "We have a grandma who lives ever so far away in the country. We don't think of her much."

"You do?" said Kate, who turned quickly, looking full of interest.

"Yes! Papa's mother is very old," added Milly. "Papa writes to her sometimes, and Mamma sends her things every Christmas. We don't know much about her, for we've only seen her once, a great long time ago. But we do care for her."

"Perhaps I shall go and see her," said Kate with a smile. "I can't get on without a grandmother. Tell me all you know about her. Is she a dear lady?"

"We only know this. She is lame and lives in the old house where Papa grew up. She has a maid named Dolly, and—that's all I can tell you about her," said Molly looking a little vexed that she could say no more of the subject that seemed to interest her cousin so much.

Kate looked surprised, but said nothing and stood looking at the fire as if turning the matter over in her mind and trying to answer the question she was too polite to ask—how could they have a grandmother and know so little about her?

At that moment, the tea bell rang, and the flock ran laughing downstairs. Kate said no more to her cousins, but she remembered the conversation and laid a plan in her resolute little mind.

ⴉ ⴉ ⴉ ⴉ ⴉ ⴉ ⴉ ⴉ ⴉ ⵣ ⴊ ⴊ ⴊ ⴊ ⴊ ⴊ ⴊ ⴊ ⴊ

Kate Reveals Her Intentions

According to her father's wish, Kate was to live for a while with the families of each of her four uncles before she decided with which she would make her home. All were anxious to have her, one because of her money, another because her great-grandfather had been a lord, a third hoped to secure her hand for the son of a close friend, while the fourth and best family loved her for herself alone.

They were worthy people, as the world goes—busy, ambitious, and prosperous; and every one, old and young, was fond of bright, pretty, generous Kate. Each family was anxious to keep her, a little jealous of the rest, and very eager to know which she would choose.

But Kate surprised them all by saying decidedly when the time came, "I would like to meet my grandma before I choose.

❦ ❦ ❦ ❦ ❦ ❦ ❦ ❦ ❦ ❦ ✻ ❦ ❦ ❦ ❦ ❦ ❦ ❦ ❦ ❦ ❦

Perhaps I should have visited her first, as she is the oldest. I believe Papa would have wished it so. At any rate, I feel I must pay her tribute before I settle anywhere."

Some of the young cousins laughed at the idea and her old-fashioned, respectful way of putting it. It was a strong contrast to their free and easy American speech. The uncles were also surprised, but they agreed to humor her whim.

Uncle George, the eldest said softly, "I should have remembered that poor Anna was mother's only daughter. Naturally, she would love to see the girl. But dear, I must warn you, it will be desperately dull. Just two old women and a quiet country town. No fun, no company. You won't want to stay long, I can assure you."

"I shall not mind the dullness for the chance to meet my grandmother," Kate replied. "Perhaps the sight of me will please her, for many say I look like my mamma."

Something in the earnest young face reminded Uncle George of the sister he had almost forgotten and recalled his own youth so pleasantly that he said, with a caress of the curly head beside him, "I believe it would. In fact, I'm sure of it. Now that you say it, I have a mind to go with you and 'pay tribute' to my mother as you have so sweetly put it."

"Oh my, but I would like to surprise her and have her all to myself for a little while. Would you mind if I went quite alone? All of you could come later if it pleases you," answered Kate.

"Of course, it will be managed exactly as you like," answered Uncle George. "I know you will bring sunshine to our old mother's life, just as you have to ours. I haven't seen her for a year, but I know she is well and comfortable, and Dolly guards her like a dragon. Give her my love, sweet Kate, and tell her we have sent her something she will value a hundred times more than the very best tea, the finest cap, or the most handsome tabby cat who ever purred."

So, in spite of the protestations of her cousins, Kate went happily off to find the grandmother whom no one else seemed to value as she did.

Meeting Grandma

Grandpa had been a farmer and lived contentedly on the old place until he died, but his four sons wanted to be something better, so they went away one after the other to make their way in the world. All worked hard, earned a good living, and forgot, as far as possible, the dull lives they had led in the old place from which they had come.

They were all good sons in their own way and had each offered his mother a home with him if she cared to come. But Grandma clung to the old home, the simple ways, and the quiet life. She thanked them gratefully, but chose to remain in the big farmhouse, empty, lonely, and plain though it was compared to the fine homes in which her sons lived.

Little by little the busy men seemed to forget their quiet, uncomplaining old mother, who spent her years thinking of

❈ ❈ ❈ ❈ ❈ ❈ ❈ ❈ ❈ ❈ ❈ ❈ ❈ ❈ ❈ ❈ ❈ ❈ ❈

them, longing to see and know their children, and hoping that one day they would remember how much she loved them.

Now and then one of her sons would pay her a hasty visit, and all sent gifts of far less value to her than one loving look, one hour of dutiful, affectionate companionship.

"If you ever want me, send and I'll come. Or if you ever need a home, remember the old place is always open, and you are always welcome here," the good old lady had told them. But they never seemed to need her and so seldom came that she concluded the old place evidently held no charming memories for them.

It was hard. But the sweet old woman bore it patiently and lived her lonely life quietly and usefully, with her faithful maid Dolly, who served and loved and supported her.

Anna, her only daughter, had married young, gone to England, and, dying early, had left her only child to her husband and his family. Among them, little Kate had grown up, knowing scarcely anything about her American relatives.

She had been the pet of her English grandmother, and, finding all her aunts to be busy, fashionable women, had longed for the tender fostering she had known and now felt as if only grandmothers could give.

With a flutter of hope and expectation, she approached the old house after the long journey was over. Leaving the luggage at the inn and accompanied only by her nurse, Bessie, Kate went up the village street and, pausing at the gate, looked with interest at the home where her mother had been born.

It was a large, old-fashioned farmhouse, with a hospitable porch and tall trees in front. Her uncles had told her that the house also had a lovely orchard in back and a hill, which grew over with luscious wild blackberries in summer and provided the perfect place for sledding in winter.

Kate noticed that all the upper windows were curtained, making the house look as if it were half asleep. At one of the lower windows, she spotted a portly puss, blinking in the sun. Just to the side and behind, she was certain she could see a cap, a regular grandmotherly old cap, with a little black bow on the back.

Something about the lonely look of the house and the pensive droop of that cap made Kate hurry on up the walk and eagerly tap the front door with the antique knocker. A brisk little old woman peered out, as if startled at the sound. Kate asked, smiling. "Does Madam Coverley live here?"

"She surely does, my dear," said the maid, "Come right in." Then throwing wide the door, she led the way down the long, wide hall and announced in a low tone to her mistress, "A lovely, young girl is here to see you, mum."

"I would love to see a young face, Dolly. Who is it?" she asked in a gentle voice.

Before Dolly could answer that she didn't know the identity of their visitor, Kate stepped straight up to the old lady with both hands out. "Grandma, can't you guess?" she asked. The first sight of her grandmother's dear face had won her heart.

Lifting her spectacles, Grandma examined her for a moment, then opened her arms without a word. In the long embrace that followed, Kate felt assured that she was welcome in the home she wanted.

"So like my Anna! And this is her little girl? God bless you, my darling! You are so good to come and see me!" said Grandma when the emotion had passed and she was able to speak again.

"Why Grandma, as soon as I knew where to find you, I was in a tizzy to come. Already I know that I will want to stay here with you as long as you will have me," Kate said, caressing her grandmother's hand affectionately.

"Then you shall never leave, for I will always want you, my darling," Grandma assured her. "Now tell me everything. It is like an angel coming to see me quite unannounced. Sit close, and let me feel sure it isn't one of the dreams I create to cheer myself when I'm feeling lonely."

Kate sat on a little stool at her grandmother's feet and, leaning on her knee, told all her little story. All the while, the old lady fed her hungry eyes with the sight of the fresh, young face, listened to the music of the child's loving voice, and felt the happy certainty that God had sent her a wonderful gift.

Kate spent the long, happy day talking and listening, looking at her new home and, to her delight, being fawned over by the two old women. Her eyes quickly read the truth of Grandma's lonely life, and her warm heart was soon flooded with tender pity for her. Kate resolved to devote herself to making her grandmother happy in her few remaining years, for at eighty, everyone should have the blessing of loving children.

To Dolly and Madam, it really did seem as if an angel had come, a singing, smiling, chattering sprite, who danced all over the old house, making blithe echoes in the silent house and brightening every room she entered. They also soon grew fond of Bessie, who welcomed their help caring for her charge.

Kate opened all the shutters and let in the sun, saying she must see which room she liked best before she settled in. She played on the old piano, which wheezed and jangled, all out of tune. But no one minded, for the girlish voice was as sweet as a lark's. She invaded Dolly's sacred kitchen and messed to her heart's content, delighting the old soul by praising her skill and begging to be taught all she knew.

She took possession of Grandma's little parlor and made it so cozy that the old lady felt as if she might have stumbled into someone else's front room. Cushioned armchairs, fur footstools, soft rugs, and delicate warm shawls appeared like magic.

Kate planted flowers in the deep, sunny window seats and hung pictures of lovely places on the oaken walls. She found a dainty workbasket for herself and placed it near Grandma's quaint one. And, best of all, she spent plenty of time in the little chair next to Grandma's rocker.

The first thing in the morning, Kate awakened her grandmother with a kiss and a cheery, "Good morning!" And all day, she hovered about her with willing hands and quick feet. Kate's loving heart returned her grandmother's love and pledged her the tender reverence, which is the beautiful tribute the young should pay the old. In the twilight, the bright head could always be found at the old woman's knee, listening to the stories of the past or making lively plans for the future. Together, they whiled away the time that had once been filled with sadness.

Kate never found it lonely, seldom wished for other society, and grew every day more certain that, in this home, she would find the cherishing she needed and do the good she hoped to do for others.

Dolly and Bessie were on capital terms; each trying to see which could sing "Little Kate's" praises loudest and spoil her quickest by unquestioning obedience to her every whim. They were a happy family, indeed! And the dull November days went by so fast that Christmas was at hand before they knew it.

❧ ❧ ❧ ❧ ❧ ❧ ❧ ❧ ❧ ❧ ❧ ❧ ❧ ❧ ❧ ❧ ❧ ❧

Kate's Christmas Surprise

All the uncles had written to ask Kate to pass the holidays with them, feeling sure that by then she would be longing for a change. But she had refused them all, thanking them for their gracious invitations. "I wish to stay with Grandma," she told them, "for she cannot go to join other people's merrymaking."

Her uncles urged, her aunts advised, and her cousins teased, but Kate denied them all, yet offended no one, for she was inspired by a grand idea and carried it out with help from Dolly and Bessie. Her grandma never suspected a thing.

"We are going to have a little Christmas fun up here among ourselves, and you mustn't know about it until we are ready. So just sit all cozy in your chair, and let me riot about as I like. I know you won't mind, and I think you'll say it is splendid when I've carried out my plan," said Kate, when the old lady wondered what she was thinking about so deeply, with her brows knit and her lips smiling.

"Very well, dear, do anything you like, and I shall enjoy it, only please don't tire yourself out by trying to do too much," said Grandma. And with that she became deaf and blind to the mysteries that went on about her.

Because she was lame and seldom left her few favorite rooms, Kate, with the help of her devoted helpers, was able to turn the house topsy-turvy. Together, the three trimmed the hall and parlor and great dining room with shining holly and evergreen, lay fires ready for kindling on the hearths that had been cold for years, and made beds fit for sleeping all over the house.

What went on in the kitchen, only Dolly could tell. But such delicious odors as stole out made Grandma sniff the air and think of merry Christmas revels long ago.

Up in her room, Kate wrote lots of letters and sent so many orders to the city that

Bessie was soon throwing up her hands. More letters came in reply, and Kate studied each one carefully with a look of pure happiness on her face.

Big bundles were left by the expressman, who came so often that the gates were left open and the lawn was full of sleigh tracks. The shops in the village were ravaged by Mistress Kate, who laid in stores of bright ribbon, toys, nuts, and all manner of delightful things.

"I really think the sweet young thing has lost her mind," said the postmaster as she flew out of the office one day with a handful of letters.

Christmas Day!

If Grandma had thought the girl out of her wits, no one could have blamed her, for on Christmas day she really did behave in the most puzzling manner.

"You are going to church with me this morning, Grandma. It's all arranged. A closed sleigh is coming for us; the sleighing is lovely, the church all trimmed out for the holidays, and I must have you see it. I shall wrap you in fur, and we will go and say our prayers together, like good girls, won't we?" said Kate, who was in an unusual flutter, her eyes shining bright, her lips full of smiles, and her feet dancing in spite of her.

"Anywhere you like, my darling," Grandma answered. "I'd start for Australia tomorrow, if you wanted me to go with you."

So they went to church, and Grandma

❄ ❄ ❄ ❄ ❄ ❄ ❄ ❄ ❄ ❄ ❄ ❄ ❄ ❄ ❄ ❄ ❄ ❄

did enjoy it, for she had many blessings to thank God for, chief among them the treasure of a dutiful, loving child. Kate tried to keep herself quiet, but the odd little flutter would not subside and seemed to get worse and worse as time went on. It increased rapidly as they drove home, and when Grandma was safe in her little parlor again, Kate's hands trembled so she could hardly tie the strings of the old lady's fancy cap.

"We must take a look in the big parlor, It is all trimmed out, and I have my presents in there. Is it ready, Dolly?" Kate asked, as the dear, old servant appeared, looking greatly excited.

"We have been quiet so long, poor Dolly doesn't know what to make of a little gayety," Grandma said smiling at her beloved companion.

"Lord bless us, my dear mum! It's all so beautiful and kind of surprising. I feel as if miracles are coming to pass again," answered Dolly, actually wiping away a tear with her best apron.

"Come, Grandma," urged Kate offering her arm. "You look so sweet and dear," she added, smoothing the soft, silken shawl about the old lady's shoulders and kissing the placid old face that beamed at her from under the festive, new cap.

"I always said Madam was the finest and dearest of women," Dolly went on. "But, do hurry, Miss Kate. That parlor door could burst open at any moment and spoil the surprise," with which mysterious remark Dolly vanished, giggling.

Across the hall they went, but at the door Kate paused, and said with a look Grandma never forgot, "I hope I have done right. I hope you will like my present and not find it too much for you. At any rate, remember that I meant to please you and give you the thing you need and long for most, my dear, sweet grandmother."

"My good child, don't be afraid. I shall like anything you do and thank you for your thoughtfulness," Grandma answered. "But, oh my! What a curious noise."

Without another word, Kate threw open the door and led Grandma in. Only a step or two—for the lady stopped short and stared about her, as if she didn't know her own best parlor. No wonder she didn't, for it was full of people, and such people! All her sons, their wives, and children rose as she came in, and turned to greet her with smiling faces. Uncle George went up and kissed her, saying, with a choke in his voice, "A merry Christmas, Mother!" and everybody echoed the words in a chorus of goodwill that went straight to the heart.

Poor Grandma could not bear it and sat down in her big chair, trembling and sobbing like a little child. Kate hung over her, fearing the surprise had been too much; but joy seldom kills, and presently, the old lady was calm enough to look up and welcome them all by stretching out her feeble hands and saying, brokenly yet heartily, "God bless you, my children! This is a merry Christmas, indeed! Now tell me all about what you've been doing. And give me names, for I don't know half the little ones."

Then Uncle George explained that it was Kate's plan, and told how she had made everyone agree to it, pleading so eloquently for Grandma that all the other plans were given up. They had arrived while she was at church and had been with difficulty kept from bursting out before the time.

"Do you like your present?" whispered Kate, quite calm and happy now that the grand surprise was safely over.

Grandma answered with a silent kiss that said more than the warmest words, and then Kate put everyone at ease by leading up the children, one by one, and introducing each with some lively speech. Everyone enjoyed this and became acquainted quickly, for Grandma thought the children the most remarkable she had ever seen. The little people soon made up their minds that an old lady who had such a very nice, big house and such a dinner waiting for them (of course, they had peeped everywhere) was a most desirable and charming grandma.

By the time the first raptures were over, Dolly and Bessie had dinner on the table, and the procession, headed by Madam proudly escorted by her eldest son, filed into the dining room where such a party had not met for years.

The dinner itself was most spectacular. Everyone partook copiously of everything, and they laughed and talked, told stories, and sang songs. The cheer they gave Grandma was almost too much for her to bear.

After that, the elders sat with Grandma in the parlor, while the younger part of the flock trooped after Kate all over the house. Fires burned everywhere, and the long un-used toys that had belonged to their father were brought out for their amusement. The big nursery was full of games, and here Bessie collected the little ones when the older boys and girls were invited by Kate to go outside for sledding. The evening ended with a cozy tea and a dance in the long hall.

The going to bed that night was the best joke of all, for though Kate's arrangements were a bit odd, everyone loved them quite well. There were many rooms, but not enough for all to have one apiece. So the uncles and aunts had the four big cham-bers, all the boys were ordered into the great playroom, where beds were made on the floor and a great fire was blazing. The nursery was devoted to the girls, and the little ones were sprinkled round wherever a snug corner was found.

How the riotous flock were ever packed away into their beds no one knows. The lads caroused until long past midnight, and no knocking on the walls of paternal boots or whispered entreaties of maternal voices through the keyholes had any effect, for it was impossible to resist the present advantages for a grand Christmas rampage.

The older girls giggled and told secrets, while the little ones tumbled into bed and went to sleep at once, quite exhausted by the festivities of this remarkable day.

Grandmother's Joy Is Complete

Grandma, down in her own cozy room, sat listening to the blithe noises with a smile on her face, for the past seemed to have come back again. It was as if her own boys and girls were once again frolicking in the rooms above her head, as they had done forty years before.

"It's all so beautiful. I can't go to bed, Dolly, and lose any of it. They'll go away to-morrow, and I may never see them again," she said, as Dolly tied on her nightcap and brought her slippers.

"Yes, you will, Mum. That dear child has made it so pleasant that they won't be able to stay away. You'll see plenty of them, if they carry out half the plans they had made. Mrs. George wants to come up and pass the summer here; Mr. Tom says he shall send his boys to school here; and every girl among them has promised Kate

❧ ❧ ❧ ❧ ❧ ❧ ❧ ❧ ❧ ❧ ❧ ❧ ❧ ❧ ❧ ❧ ❧ ❧ ❧

to make her a long visit. You'll never be lonely again, Mum."

"Thank God for that!" Grandma said bowing her head to acknowledge that she had received a great blessing. "Dolly, I want to go and look at those children. It seems so like a dream to have them here, I must be sure of it," said Grandma, folding her wrapper about her, and getting up with great decision.

"Oh my, Mum," Dolly protested. "You haven't been up those stairs in months. The dears are just fine, sleeping warm as toast."

But Grandma would go, so Dolly gave her an arm, and together the two dear friends hobbled up the wide stairs and peeped in at the precious children. The lads looked like a camp of weary warriors reposing after a victory, and Grandma went laughing away when she had taken a proud survey of this promising portion of the younger generation.

The nursery was like a little convent full of rosy nuns sleeping peacefully, while a picture of Saint Agnes, with her lamb, smiled on them from the wall. The firelight flickered over the white figures and sweet faces, as if the sight were too fair to be lost in darkness. The little ones lay about, looking like little Cupids with sugar hearts and faded roses still clutched in their chubby hands.

"My darlings!" whispered Grandma, lingering fondly over them to cover a pair of rosy feet, put back a pile of tumbled curls, or kiss a little mouth still smiling in its sleep.

But when she came to the coldest corner of the room, where Kate lay on the hardest mattress, under the thinnest quilt, the old lady's eyes were full of tender tears. Forgetting the stiff joints that bent so painfully, she knelt slowly down and, putting her arms about the girl, blessed her in silence for the happiness she had given one old heart.

Kate woke at once and started up, exclaiming with a smile, "Why Grandma, I was dreaming about an angel, and you look like one with your white gown and silvery hair!"

"No, dear, you are the angel in this house. How can I ever give you up?" an-

❅ ❅ ❅ ❅ ❅ ❅ ❅ ❅ ❅ ❅ ❅ ❅ ❅ ❅ ❅ ❅ ❅ ❅

swered Madam, holding fast the treasure that came to her so late.

"You never need to, Grandma, for I have made my choice."

The End

BOOK ✳ TWO

What Love Can Do

C. M. DUDASH

What Love Can Do

The small room had nothing in it but a bed, two chairs, and a big chest. A few little gowns hung on the wall, and the only picture was the wintry sky, sparkling with stars, framed by the uncurtained window. But the moon, pausing to peep, saw something touching and heard something pleasant. Two heads in little round night-caps lay on one pillow, two pairs of wide-awake blue eyes stared up at the light, and two tongues were going like bell clappers.

"I'm so glad we finished our shirts in time! It seemed as though we never should, and I don't think six cents is half enough for a great red flannel shirt with four buttonholes, do you?" said one voice rather wearily.

"No; but then we each made four, and

fifty cents is a good deal of money. Are you sorry we didn't keep our quarters for ourselves?" asked the other voice with an undertone of regret.

"Yes, I am, till I think how pleased the children will be with our tree, for they don't expect anything at all and will be so surprised. I wish we had more toys to put on it, for it looks so small and mean with only three or four things hanging from it."

"Oh, it won't hold anymore, so I wouldn't worry about it. The toys are very red and yellow, and I guess the babies won't know how cheap they are but like them as much as if they cost heaps of money."

With that brave, cheery reply, the four blue eyes turned toward the chest under the window, and the kind moon did her best to light up the tiny tree standing there. A very pitiful little tree it was—only a branch of hemlock in an old flowerpot propped up with bits of coal and hung with a few penny toys earned by the patient fingers of the elder sisters that the younger ones should not be disappointed.

But in spite of the magical moonlight, the broken branch, with its scanty supply of fruit, looked pathetically poor, and one pair of eyes filled slowly with tears, while the other pair lost their happy look as if a cloud had covered the moonbeams.

"Are you crying, Dolly?"

"Not much, Grace."

"What makes you sad, dear?"

"I didn't know how poor we were till I saw the tree, and then I couldn't help it," sobbed the elder sister, for at twelve she already knew something of the cares of poverty and missed the happiness that seemed to vanish out of all their lives when Father died.

"It's dreadful! I never thought we'd have to earn our tree and only be able to get a broken branch, after all, with nothing on it but three sticks of candy, two squeaking dogs, a red cow, and an ugly bird with one feather in its tail." Overcome by a sudden sense of destitution, Grace sobbed even more despairingly than Dolly.

"Hush, dear; we must cry softly or Mother will hear and come up, and then we shall have to tell. You know we said we wouldn't mind not having any Christmas, she seemed so sorry about it."

"I *must* cry, but I'll be quiet about it."

So the two heads went under the pillow for a few minutes and not a sound betrayed them as the sisters cried softly in one another's arms, lest Mother should discover that they were no longer careless children, but brave young creatures trying to bear their share of poverty cheerfully.

When the shower was over, the faces came out shining like roses after rain, and the voices went on again as before.

"Don't you wish there really was a Santa Claus who knew what we wanted and would come and put two silver half dollars in our stockings, so we could go to see Puss 'n Boots at the theatre tomorrow afternoon?"

"Yes, indeed; but we didn't hang up any stockings anyway, you know, because Mother had nothing to put in them. It does seem as if rich people might think of the poor now and then. Such small considerations would help us feel remembered, and it couldn't be much trouble to take two small girls to the play."

"*I* shall remember to do something when I'm rich, like Mr. Chrome and Miss Kent. I shall go round every Christmas with a big basket of goodies and give all the poor children some."

"Perhaps if we sew ever so many flannel shirts we may be rich by-and-by. I should give Mother a new bonnet first of all, for I heard Miss Kent say no lady would wear such a shabby one. Mrs. Smith said fine bonnets didn't make real ladies, though. I like her best, but I do want a locket like Miss Kent's."

"I should give Mother some new rain shoes, and then I should buy a white apron with frills like Miss Kent's and bring home nice bunches of grapes and good things to eat, as Mr. Chrome does. I often smell them, but he never gives me any. He only says, 'Hullo, little chick,' and I'd rather have oranges anytime."

"It will take us a long while to get rich, I'm afraid. It makes me tired to think of it. I guess we'd better go to sleep now, dear."

"Good night, Dolly."

"Good night, Grace."

They kissed each other softly, a nestling sound followed, and presently the little sisters lay fast asleep cheek-against-cheek on the pillow wet with their tears, never dreaming of what was going to happen to them tomorrow.

Now Miss Kent's room was next to theirs, and as she sat sewing she could hear the children's talk, for they had soon forgotten to whisper. At first she smiled, then she looked sober, and when the prattle ceased, she said to herself, as she glanced about her pleasant chamber: "Poor little things! They think I'm rich and envy me when I'm only a ladies' hatmaker earning my living. I ought to have taken more notice of them, for their mother does have a hard time, I fancy, but never complains.

"I'm sorry they heard what I said, and if I knew how to do it without offending her, I'd trim a nice bonnet for a Christmas gift, for their mother is a dear lady in spite of her poor clothes. Perhaps I can give the children something they want any-how—and I will! The idea of those mites making a fortune out of shirts at six cents apiece!"

Miss Kent laughed at the innocent delu-sion but sympathized with her little neigh-bors, for she knew all about hard .times. She had good wages now but spent them on herself and liked to be considered fine rather than neat. Still, she was a good-hearted young woman and what she had overheard set her to thinking soberly about what she might do.

"If I hadn't spent all my money on my dress for the party tomorrow night, I'd give each of them a half dollar. As I cannot, I'll hunt up the other things they wanted, for it's a shame they shouldn't have a bit of Christmas when they have tried so hard to please other little ones."

As she spoke, she stirred about her room and soon had a white apron, an old carnelian heart on a fresh blue ribbon, and two papers of bonbons ready. As no stock-ings were hung up, she laid a clean towel on the floor before the door and spread forth the small gifts to look their best.

Miss Kent was so busy that she did not hear a step come quietly upstairs, and Mr. Chrome, the artist, peeped at her through the balusters, wondering what she was about. He soon saw and watched her with pleasure, thinking that she never looked prettier than now.

Presently, she caught him at it and hastened to explain, telling what she had heard and how she was trying to atone for her past neglect of these young neighbors. Then she said good night and both went into their rooms—she to sleep happily, and he to meditate thoughtfully.

His eye kept turning to some bundles that lay on his table as if the story he had heard suggested how he might follow Miss Kent's example. I rather think he would not have disturbed himself if he had not heard the story told in such a soft voice, with a pair of bright eyes full of pity looking into his; for little girls were not particularly interesting to him, and he was usually too tired to notice the industrious creatures who toiled up and down stairs on various errands. He was busy himself after all.

Now that he knew something of their small troubles, he felt as if it would please Miss Kent and be a good joke to do his share of the pretty work she had begun.

So presently he jumped up, and, opening his parcels, took out two oranges and two bunches of grapes; then he looked up two silver half dollars, and stealing into the hall, laid the fruit upon the towel, and the money atop the oranges. This addition improved the display very much, and Mr. Chrome was stealing back, well pleased, when his eye fell on Miss Kent's door, and he said to himself: "She too shall have a little surprise, for she is a dear, kind-hearted soul."

In his room was a prettily painted plate, and this he filled with green and purple grapes, tucked a sentimental note underneath, and leaving it on her threshold, crept away as stealthily as a burglar.

The house was very quiet when Mrs. Smith, the landlady, came to turn off the

gas. "Well, upon my word, here's fine do-
ings, to be sure!" she said when she saw
the state of the upper hall. "Now I wouldn't
have thought it of Miss Kent, she is such a
giddy girl, nor of Mr. Chrome, he is so busy
with his own affairs. I meant to give those
children each a cake tomorrow; they are
such good little things. I'll run down and
get them now, as my contribution to this
fine display."

Away trotted Mrs. Smith to her pantry
and picked out a couple of tempting
cakes, shaped like hearts and full of plums.
There was a goodly array of pies on the
shelves, and she took two of them, saying,
as she climbed the stairs again, "They remembered the children, so I'll remember
them and have my share of the fun."

So up went the pies, for Mrs. Smith had
not much to give, and her spirit was generous, though her pastry was not of the best.
It looked very droll to see pies sitting about
on the thresholds of closed doors, but the
cakes were quite elegant and filled up the
corners of the towel handsomely, for the
apron lay in the middle, with oranges right

and left, like two sentinels in orange uniform.

It was very late when the flicker of a candle came upstairs and a pale lady, with a sweet sad face, appeared, bringing a pair of red and a pair of blue mittens for her Dolly and Grace. Poor Mrs. Blake did have a hard time, for she stood all day in a great store that she might earn bread for the poor children who stayed at home and took care of one another.

Her heart was heavy that night, because it was the first Christmas she had ever known without gifts and festivity of some sort. But Petkin, the youngest child, had been ill, times were hard, the little mouths gaped for food like the bills of hungry birds, and there was no tender mate to help fill them.

The angels hovering about the dingy hall just then must have seen the mother's tired face brighten beautifully when she discovered the gifts, and found that her little helpers had been so kindly remembered. Something more brilliant than the mock diamonds in Miss Kent's best earrings fell and glittered on the dusty floor as Mrs.

Blake added the mittens to the other things and went to her lonely room again, smiling as she thought how she could thank all the contributors in a pleasant and simple way.

Her windows were full of flowers, for the delicate tastes of the poor lady found great comfort in their beauty. "I have nothing else to give, and these will show how grateful I am," she said as she rejoiced that the scarlet geraniums were so full of gay clusters, the white chrysanthemum stars were all out, and the pink roses at their loveliest.

The flowers slept now, dreaming of a sunny morrow as they sat safely sheltered from the bitter cold. But that night was their last, for a gentle hand cut them all, and soon three pretty nosegays stood in a glass, waiting for dawn, to be laid at three doors, with a few grateful words which would surprise and delight the receivers, for flowers were rare in those hardworking lives, and kind deeds often come back to the givers in fairer shapes than they go.

Now one would think that there had

been gifts enough, and no more could possibly arrive, since all had added his or her mite except Betsey, the maid, who was off on a holiday, and the babies fast asleep in their trundle bed with nothing to give but love and kisses. Nobody dreamed that the old cat would take it into her head that her kittens were in danger, because Mrs. Smith had said she thought they were nearly old enough to be given away. But the cat must have understood, for when all was dark and still, the anxious mother went patting upstairs to the children's door, meaning to hide her babies under their bed, sure they would be saved destruction. Mrs. Blake had shut the door, however, so poor Puss was disappointed; but finding a soft, clean spot among a variety of curious articles, she laid her kits there and kept them warm all night, with her head pillowed on the blue mittens.

In the cold morning Dolly and Grace got up and scrambled into their clothes, not with joyful haste to see what their stockings held, for they had none, but because they had the little ones to dress while Mother got the breakfast.

Dolly opened the door and started back with a cry of astonishment at the lovely spectacle before her. The other people had taken in their gifts, so nothing destroyed the magnificent effect of the treasures so curiously collected in the night. Puss had left her kits asleep and gone down to get her own breakfast; and there, in the middle of the ruffled apron, as if in a dainty cradle, lay the two Maltese darlings, with white bibs and boots on, and white tips to the tiny tails curled round their little noses.

Grace and Dolly could only clasp their hands and look in rapturous silence for a minute; then they went down on their knees and reveled in the unexpected richness before them.

"I do believe angels must have heard us, for here is everything we wanted," said Dolly, holding the carnelian heart in one hand and the plumy one in the other.

"How can we ever explain this, for we didn't mention kittens, but we wanted one, and here are two darlings," cried Grace, almost purring with delight as the downy bunches unrolled and gaped till their bits of pink tongues were visible.

"Mrs. Smith must have been one angel, I guess, and Miss Kent was another, for that is her apron. I shouldn't wonder if Mr. Chrome gave us the oranges and the money; men always have lots, and his name is on this bit of paper," said Dolly.

"Oh, I'm so glad! Now we shall have a Christmas like other people, and I'll never say again that rich folks don't remember poor folks. Come and show all our treasures to Mother and the babies; they must have some," answered Grace, feeling that the world was all right and life not half as hard as she thought it last night.

Shrieks of delight greeted the sisters, and all that morning there was joy and feasting in Mrs. Blake's room; and in the afternoon Dolly and Grace went to the theatre and actually saw *Puss 'n Boots,* for their mother insisted on their going, having discovered how the hard-earned quarters had been spent. This was such unhoped-for bliss they could hardly believe it and kept smiling at one another so brightly that people wondered who the happy girls in the shabby cloaks could be who clapped their new mittens so heartily and laughed till it was better than music to hear them.

This was a remarkable Christmas Day, and they long remembered it; for while they were absorbed in the fortunes of the Marquis of Carabas and the funny cat, who tucked his tail in his belt, washed his face so awkwardly, and didn't know how to purr, strange things were happening at home, and more surprises were in store for Dolly and Grace.

You see, when people once begin to do kindnesses, it is so easy and pleasant, they find it hard to leave off; and sometimes it beautifies them so that they find they love one another very much—as Mr. Chrome and Miss Kent discovered that wondrous day.

They were very jolly at dinner and talked a good deal about the Blakes, who ate in their own rooms. Miss Kent told what the children said, and it touched the soft spot in all their hearts to hear about the red shirts, though they laughed at Grace's lament over the bird with only one feather in its tail.

"I'd give them a better tree if I had any place to put it and knew how to trim it up," said Mr. Chrome, with a sudden burst of generosity, which so pleased Miss Kent that her eyes shone like Christmas candles.

"Put it in the back parlor. All the Browns are away for a week, and we'll help you trim it—won't we, my dear?" cried Mrs. Smith warmly; for she saw that he was in a sociable mood and thought it a pity the Blakes should not profit by it.

"Yes, indeed, I should like it of all things, and it needn't cost much, for I have some skill in trimming, as you know." And Miss Kent looked so gay and pretty as she spoke that Mr. Chrome made up his mind that millinery must be a delightful occupation.

"Come on then, ladies, and we'll have a little fun. I'm a lonely old bachelor with nowhere to go today, and I'd like to be in good company and have a good time."

They had it, I assure you, for they all fell

to work as busy as bees, flying and buzzing about with much laughter as they worked their pleasant miracle. Mr. Chrome acted more like a father of a large family than a crusty bachelor. Miss Kent's skillful fingers flew as they never did before, and Mrs. Smith trotted up and down as briskly as if she were sixteen instead of being a stout, elderly woman of seventy.

The children were so full of the play and telling about it that they forgot their tree till after supper, but when they went to look for it, they found it gone and in its place a great paper hand with one finger pointing downstairs, and on it these mysterious words in red: "Look in the Browns' back parlor!"

At the door of that interesting apartment they found their mother with Will and Petkin, for another hand had suddenly appeared to them pointing up. The door flew open quite as if it were a fairy play, and they went in to find a pretty tree planted in a red box on the center table, lighted with candles, hung with gilded nuts, red apples, gay bonbons, and a gift for each child.

Mr. Chrome was hidden behind one folding door, and stout Mrs. Smith squeezed behind the other, and they both thought it a great improvement upon an old-fashioned Santa Claus to have Miss Kent, in her new white dress, with Mrs. Blake's roses in her hair, step forward as the children gazed in silent rapture, and with a few sweet words welcome them to surprises their friends had made.

There were many Christmas trees in the city that night, but none that gave such hearty pleasures as the one which so magically took the place of the broken branch and its few poor toys. They were all there, however, and Dolly and Grace were immensely pleased to see that, of all their gifts, Petkin chose the forlorn bird to carry to bed with her, the one yellow feather being just to her taste.

Mrs. Blake put on her neat bonnet and was so gratified that Miss Kent thought it the most successful one she ever trimmed. She was well paid for it by the thanks of one neighbor and the admiration of another; for when she went to her party, Mr.

Chrome went with her and said something on the way which made her heart dance more lightly than her feet that night.

Good Mrs. Smith felt that her house had covered itself with glory by this event, and Dolly and Grace declared that it was the most perfect and delightful surprise party ever seen.

It was all over by nine o'clock and with goodnight kisses for everyone, the little girls climbed up to bed laden with treasures and too happy for many words. But as they tied their round caps Dolly said, thoughtfully: "On the whole, I think it's rather nice to be poor when people are kind to you."

"Well, I'd rather be rich, but if I can't be, it is very good fun to have Christmas trees like this one," answered Grace truthfully, never guessing that they had planted the seed from which the little pine tree grew so quickly and beautifully.

When the moon came to look in at the window on her nightly round, two smiling faces lay on the pillow, which was no longer wet with tears, but rather knobby

with the mine of riches hidden underneath—firstfruits of the neighborly friendship which flourished in that house until
another and a merrier Christmas came.

The End

BOOK ✻ THREE

Gwen's Adventure in the Snow

Gwen's Adventure in the Snow

"Gwen, it looks so much like snow I think it would be wise to put off your sleighing party," said Mrs. Arnold, fretfully looking out at the heavy sky and streets still drifted by the last winter storm.

"Not before night, Mamma. We don't mind its being cloudy; we like it, because the sun makes the snow so dazzling when we get out of town. We can't give it up now, for here comes Patrick with the boys." And Gwen ran down to welcome the big sleigh, which just then drove up with four jolly lads skirmishing about inside.

"Come on!" called Mark, her brother, knocking his friends right and left to make room for the four girls who were to complete the party.

"What do you think of the weather, Patrick?" asked Mrs. Arnold from the window, still undecided about the wisdom of letting her flock go off alone, Papa having been called away after the plan had been made.

"Faith, Ma'am, it's an elegant day, if not fer the wind that's a trifle cold for the nose. I'll have me eye on the children, Ma'am, and there'll be no trouble at all, at all," replied the faithful coachman, lifting a red muffler around his face and patting little Gus on the shoulder as he sat proudly on the high seat holding the whip.

"Be careful, dears, and come home early."

With which parting caution Mamma shut the window and watched the young folks drive gaily away, little dreaming what would happen before they got back.

The wind was more than a trifle cold, for when they got out of the city it blew across the open country in bitter blasts and made the bright little noses almost as red as the driver's whose face jutted cheerfully in the wind. The truth is, Patrick just loved driving at anytime, whether there was any danger or not.

When the lively crew had gotten out into the open country, the coachman stopped near a snowdrift. The lads enjoyed themselves immensely snowballing one another, for the drifts were still fresh enough to furnish soft snow; and Mark, Bob, and Tony had many a friendly tussle in it as they went up hills or paused to rest the horses after a swift trot along a level bit of road.

Little Gus helped drive till his hands were benumbed in spite of the new red mittens, and he had to descend among the girls, who were cuddled cozily under the warm robes, telling secrets, eating candy, and laughing at the older boys' pranks.

Sixteen-year-old Gwendoline was matron of the party and kept excellent order among the girls, for Ruth and Alice were nearly her own age and Rita a most obedient younger sister.

"I say, Gwen, we are going to stop at the summerhouse on the way home and get some nuts for this evening. Papa said we might, and some of the big walnuts too.

I've got baskets, and while we fellows fill them, you girls can look round the house," said Mark when the exhausted young gentlemen returned to their seats.

"That will be nice. I want to get some books, and Rita has been very anxious about one of her dolls, which she is sure was left in the nursery closet. If we are going to stop, we ought to be turning back, Pat, for it is beginning to snow and will be dark early," warned Gwen, suddenly realizing that great flakes were fast whitening the roads and the wind had risen to a gale.

"Sure, and I will, miss dear, as soon as I can. But it's round a good bit we must go, for I couldn't be turning the sleigh without upsettin' the whole of you; it's that drifted. Rest easy, and I'll fetch up at the old place in half an hour," said Pat, who had lost his way and wouldn't own it, being embarrassed at the turn of events.

On they went again, with the wind at their backs, caring little for the snow that now fell fast, or the gathering twilight, since they were going toward home, they thought. It was a very long half-hour before Pat brought them to the country house, which was shut up for the winter. With difficulty they ploughed their way up to the steps and scrambled on to the piazza, where they danced about to warm their feet till Mark unlocked the door and let them in, leaving Pat to enjoy a doze on his seat.

"Make haste, boys; it is cold and dark here, and we must get home. Mamma will be so anxious, and it really is going to be a bad storm," said Gwen, whose spirits were damped by the gloom of the old house, and who felt her responsibility, having promised to be home early.

Off went the boys to attic and cellar, being obliged to light the lantern left there for the use of whoever came now and then to inspect the premises. The girls, having found books and a doll, sat upon the rolled up carpets or peeped about at the once gay and hospitable rooms, now looking very empty and desolate with piled-up furniture, shuttered windows, and fireless hearths.

"If we were going to stay long, I'd have a fire in the library. Papa often does when he comes out to keep the books from moldering," began Gwen, but was interrupted by a shout from without, and—running to the door—saw Pat picking himself out of a drift while the horses went galloping down the avenue at full speed.

"Be jabbers, the horses gave a jump when that fallin' branch struck 'em, and out I went, being taken off guard by their fright. Don't worry now, dear! I'll fetch 'em back in a jiffy. Stop still till I come, and keep those boys busy."

With a blow to settle his hat, Patrick trotted gallantly away into the storm, and the girls went in to tell the exciting news to the lads, who came whooping back from their search with baskets of nuts and apples.

"Here's a go!" cried Mark. "Pat will run halfway to town before he catches the horses, and we are in for an hour or two at least."

"Then do make a fire, for we shall die of cold if we have to wait long," begged Gwen, rubbing Rita's cold hands and looking anxiously at little Gus, who was about making up his mind to cry.

"So we will, and be jolly till Patrick catches the horses. Camp down, girls, and you fellows, come and hold the lantern while I get wood and stuff. It is so confoundedly dark, I shall break my neck down the shed steps." And Mark led the way to the library where the carpet still remained and comfortable chairs and sofas invited the chilly visitors to rest.

"How can you light your fire when you get the wood?" asked Ruth, a practical damsel, who looked well after her own creature comforts and was longing for a warm supper.

"Papa hides the matches in a tin box, so the mice won't get at them. Here they are, and two or three bits of candle for the sticks on the chimney piece, if he forgets to have the lantern trimmed. Now we will light up and look cozy when the boys come back."

And producing the box from under a sofa cushion, Gwen cheered the hearts of all by lighting two candles, rolling up the chairs, and making ready to be comfortable. Thoughtful Alice went to see if Pat was returning and found a buffalo robe lying on the steps. Returning with this, she reported that there was no sign of the runaways and advised them to make ready for a long stay.

"How Mamma will worry!" thought Gwen, but made light of the affair, because she saw Rita looked timid, and Gus shivered till his teeth chattered.

"We will have a nice time and play we are shipwrecked people or Artic explorers. Here comes the captain and the sailors with supplies of food, so we can thaw our pemmican and warm our feet. Gus shall be the little Inuit boy, all dressed in fur, as he is in the picture we have at home," she said, wrapping the child in the robe and putting her own sealskin cap on his head to divert his mind.

"Here we are! Now for a jolly blaze, boys; and if Pat doesn't come back, we can have our fun here instead of home," cried Mark, well pleased with the adventure as were his mates.

So they fell to work, and soon a bright fire was lighting up the room with its cheerful shine, and the children gathered about it, quite careless of the storm raging without and sure that Pat would come shortly.

❧ ❧ ❧ ❧ ❧ ❧ ❧ ❧ ❧ ✸ ❧ ❧ ❧ ❧ ❧ ❧ ❧ ❧ ❧

"I'm hungry," complained Gus as soon as he was warm.

"So am I," added Rita from the rug where the two little ones sat basting themselves.

"Eat an apple," said Mark.

"They are so hard and cold I don't like them," began Gus.

"Roast some!" cried Ruth.

"And crack nuts," suggested Alice. "Pity we can't cook something in real camp style, it would be such fun," said Tony, who had spent weeks on Monadnock living upon the supplies he and his party tugged up the mountain on their backs.

"We shall not have time for anything but what we have. Put down your apples and crack away, or we shall be obliged to leave them," advised Gwen, coming back from an observation at the front door with an anxious line on her forehead; for the storm was rapidly increasing, and there was no sign of Pat or the horses.

The rest were in high glee, and an hour or two slipped quickly away as they enjoyed the impromptu feast and played games. Gus recalled them to the discomforts of their situation by saying with a yawn and a whimper: "I'm so sleepy! I want my own bed and Mamma."

"So do I!" echoed Rita, who had been nodding for some time and longed to lie down and sleep comfortably anywhere.

"Almost eight o'clock! By Jove, Pat sure is taking his time. I wonder if he has gotten into trouble? We can't do anything and may as well keep quiet here," said Mark, looking at his watch and beginning to understand that the joke was rather a serious one.

"Better make a night of it and all go to sleep. Pat can wake us up when he comes. The cold makes a fellow so drowsy." And Bob gave a stretch that nearly rent him asunder.

"I will let the children nap on the sofa. They are so tired of waiting and may as well amuse themselves in that way as in fretting. Come, Gus and Rita, each take a pillow, and I'll cover you up with my shawl."

Gwen made the little ones comfortable, and they were off in five minutes. The others kept up bravely till nine o'clock, then the bits of candles were burnt out, the stories all told, nuts and apples had lost their charm, and weariness and hunger caused spirits to fail perceptibly.

"I've eaten five walnuts, and yet I want more. Something filling and good. Can't we catch a rabbit and roast him?" proposed Bob, who was a hearty lad and was ravenous by this time.

"Isn't there anything in the house?" asked Ruth, who dared not eat nuts for fear of indigestion.

"Not a thing that I know of except a few pickles in the storeroom; we had so many Mamma left some here," answered Gwen, resolving to provision the house before she left it another autumn.

"Pickles alone are a rather sour feed. If we only had a biscuit now, they wouldn't be so bad for relish," said Tony, with the air of a man who had known what it was to live on burnt bean soup and rye flapjacks for a week.

"I saw a keg of soft soap in the shed. How would that go with the pickles?" suggested Bob, who felt equal to the biggest and acidest cucumber ever grown.

"Oh, ugh! Mamma knew an old lady who actually did eat soft soap and cream for her complexion," put in Alice, whose own fresh face looked as if she had tried the same distasteful remedy.

The boys laughed, and Mark, who felt that hospitality required him to do something for his guests, said briskly: "Let us go on a foraging expedition while the lamp holds out to burn, for the old lantern is almost gone and then we are done for. Come on, Bob. Your sharp nose will smell out food, if there is any."

"Don't set the house afire, and bring more wood when you come, for we must have light of some kind in this spooky place," called Gwen, with a sigh, wishing every one of them were safely at home and abed.

A great trampling of boots, slamming of doors, and shouting of voices followed the departure of the boys, as well as a crash, a howl, and then a roar of laughter, as Bob fell down the cellar stairs, having opened the door in search of food and poked his nose in too far. Presently, they came back, very dusty, cobwebby, and cold, but triumphantly bearing a droll collection of trophies. Mark had a piece of board and the lantern, Tony a big wooden box and a tin pail, and Bob fondly embraced a pickle jar and a tumbler of jelly which had been forgotten on a high shelf in the storeroom.

"Meal, pickles, jam, and boards. What a mess and what are we to do with it all?" cried the girls, much amused at the result of the expedition.

"Can any of you make a hoe cake?" demanded Mark.

"No, indeed! I can make caramels and coconut cakes," said Ruth proudly.

"I can make good toast and tea," added Alice.

"I can't cook anything," confessed Gwen, who was unusually accomplished in French, German, and music.

"That's not very promising," said Mark. "Take hold, Tony; you are the chap for me." And Mark disrespectfully turned his back on the young ladies, who could only sit and watch the lads work.

"He can't do anything without water," whispered Ruth.

"Or salt," answered Alice.

"Or a pan to bake in," added Gwen, and then the girls smiled at the dilemma they foresaw.

But Tony was equal to the occasion and calmly went on with his tasks, while Mark arranged the fire and Bob opened the pickles. First, the new cook filled the pail with snow till enough was melted to wet the meal brought in the wooden box. This mixture was stirred with a pine stick till thick enough, then spread on the board and set up before the bed of coals to brown.

"It never will bake in the world." "He can't turn it, so it won't be done on both sides." "Won't be fit to eat anyway!" And with these dark hints the girls consoled themselves for their want of skill.

But the bread did bake a nice brown; Tony did turn it neatly with his jack-knife and the stick. And when it was done and cut into bits, smeared with jelly, and passed around on an old atlas, everyone said: "It really does taste good!"

Two more bakings were made and eaten with pickles for a change. Then all were satisfied, and after a vote of thanks to Tony, they began to think of sleep.

✶ ✶ ✶ ✶ ✶ ✶ ✶ ✶ ✶ ✶ ✶ ✶ ✶ ✶ ✶ ✶ ✶ ✶ ✶

"Pat has gone home and told them we are all right, and Mamma knows we can manage here well enough for one night; so don't worry, Gwen, but take a nap and I'll lie on the rug and see to the fire."

Mark's happy-go-lucky way of taking things did not convince his sister; but, as she could do nothing, she submitted and made her friends as comfortable as she could.

All had plenty of wraps, so the girls nestled into the three large chairs, and Bob and Tony rolled themselves up in the robe, with their feet to the fire, and were soon snoring like weary hunters. Mark pillowed his head on a log and was sound asleep in ten minutes in spite of his promise to be sentinel.

Gwen's chair was the least easy of the three, and she could not forget herself like the rest, but sat wide awake, watching the blaze, counting the hours, and wondering why no one came to them.

The wind blew fiercely, the snow beat against the blinds, mice scuttled about inside the walls, and now and then a branch fell upon the roof with a crash. Weary, yet excited, the poor girl imagined all sorts of mishaps to Pat and the horses, recalled various ghost stories she had heard, and wondered if it was on such a night as this that a neighbor's house had been robbed. So nervous did she get at last that she covered up her face and resolutely began to count to a thousand, feeling that anything was better than having to wake Mark and own she was frightened.

Before she knew it, she fell into a drowse and dreamed that they were all cast away on an iceberg and a polar bear was coming up to devour Gus, who innocently called to the big white dog and waited to caress him.

"A bear! A bear! Oh, boys, save him!" murmured Gwen in her sleep, and the sound of her own distressed voice waked her.

The fire was nearly out, for she had slept longer than she knew. The room was full of shadows, and the storm seemed to have died away. In the silence which now reigned, unbroken even by a snore, Gwen heard a sound that made her start and tremble. Someone was coming softly up the back stairs. All the outer doors were locked, she was sure; all the boys lay in their places, for she could see and count the three long figures and little Gus in a bunch on the sofa. The girls had not stirred, and this was no mouse's scamper, but a slow and careful tread, stealing nearer and nearer to the study door, left ajar when the last load of wood was brought in.

Pat would knock or ring, and Papa would speak, so that we might not be scared. I want to scream, but I won't till I see that it really is someone, thought Gwen, while her heart beat fast, and her eyes were fixed on the door, straining to see through the gloom.

The steps drew nearer, paused on the threshold, and then a head appeared as the door noiselessly swung wider open. It was a man in a fur cap, but it was neither Papa nor Pat nor Uncle Ed. Poor Gwen would have called out then, but her voice was gone; and she could only lie back, looking mute and motionless.

A tiny spire of flame sprung up and flickered for a moment on the tall figure in the doorway, a big man with a beard, and in his hand something that glittered. *Is it a pistol or dagger or a dark lantern?* thought the girl, as the glimmer died away, and the shadows returned to terrify her.

The man seemed to look about him keenly for a moment, then vanished, and the steps went down the hall to the front door, which was opened from within and someone admitted quietly. Whispers were heard, and then feet approached again, accompanied by a gleam of light.

Now I must scream! thought Gwen, and scream she did with all her might, as two men entered, one carrying a lantern, the other a bright tin can.

"Boys! Robbers! Fire! Tramps! Oh, do wake up!" cried Gwen, frantically pulling Mark by the hair, and Bob and Tony by the legs, as the quickest way of rousing them.

Then there was a scene! The boys sprung up and rubbed their eyes, the girls hid theirs and began to shriek, while the burglars laughed aloud, and poor Gwen, quite worn out, fainted away on the rug. It was all over in a minute, however, for Mark had his wits about him, and his first glance at the man with the lantern allayed his fears.

"Hullo, Uncle Ed! We are all right. Got tired of waiting for you, so we went to sleep."

"Stop screaming, girls, and quiet those children! Poor little Gwen is badly frightened. Get some snow, Tom, while I pick her up," commanded the uncle, and order was soon established.

The boys were all right at once, and Ruth and Alice devoted themselves to the children, who were very cross and sleepy in spite of their fright. Gwen was herself in a moment and so ashamed of her scare that she was glad there was no more light to betray her pale cheeks.

"I should have known you, uncle, at once; but to see a strange man startled me, and he didn't speak, and I thought that can was a pistol," stammered Gwen, when she had collected her wits a little.

"Why, that's my old friend and captain, Tom May. Don't you remember him, child? He thought you were all asleep, so he crept out to tell me and let me in."

ᴊ ᴊ ᴊ ᴊ ᴊ ᴊ ᴊ ᴊ ᴊ ᴥ ᴊ ᴊ ᴊ ᴊ ᴊ ᴊ ᴊ ᴊ

"How did he get in himself?" asked Gwen, glad to turn the conversation.

"Found the shed door open and surprised the camp by a flank movement. You wouldn't do for guard duty, boys," laughed Captain Tom, enjoying the dismay of the lads.

"Oh, thunder! I forgot to bolt it when we first went for the wood. Had to open it, the place was so dark," muttered Bob, much disgusted.

"Where's Pat?" asked Tony, with great presence of mind, feeling anxious to shift the blame to his broad shoulders.

Uncle Ed shook the snow from his hair and clothes, and, poking up the fire, leisurely sat down and took Gus on his knee: "The truth is, Pat got a terrible fright and nearly lost his wits. In the first place, after he found the horses, he found they were still a bit wild. Then he got on the sleigh and promptly lost his way again; it was snowing so hard. Then he hit a ditch and got tumbled overboard and let the horses go. He floundered after them for a mile or two; then lost his bearings in the storm again, tripped over a stump and lay senseless until we found him, for we were out by then.

"The animals were stopped at a cross-roads, and we got them and Pat back home. Then your mother remembered that you had mentioned stopping here, and we fitted out a new craft and set sail for a long voyage. Your father was away, so Tom volunteered, and here we are."

"A jolly lark! Now let us go home and go to bed," proposed Mark sensibly.

"Isn't it almost morning?" asked Tony, who had been sleeping like a dormouse.

"Just eleven. Now pack up and let us be off. The storm is over, the moon coming out, and we shall find a good supper waiting for the loved and lost. Bear a hand, Tom, and ship this little duffer, for he's off again."

Uncle Ed put Gus into the captain's arms, and, taking Rita himself, led the way to the sleigh which stood at the door. In they all bundled, and after making the house safe, off they went, feeling that they had had a pretty good time on the whole.

"I will learn cooking and courage, before I try camping out again," resolved Gwen.

⚘ ⚘ ⚘ ⚘ ⚘ ⚘ ⚘ ⚘ ⚘ ⚘ ⚘ ⚘ ⚘ ⚘ ⚘ ⚘ ⚘

Really a brave girl, she was determined to learn from her adventure and add to her skills not only languages and music but also camping out!

The End

THE
EDITOR'S
NOTES

THE EDITOR'S NOTES

Kate's Choice—

Louisa May Alcott never wrote her autobiography, but she did use her personal experiences to give authenticity to her stories. When she traveled to England in 1870, she found she was treated as something of a celebrity. It was her predisposition to like the English, and she set some of her stories in London.

In "Kate's Choice" she uses her experience to draw the character of Kate, who is someone intensely aware of family connections, English, and eager to do the right thing. Though Kate is new to this country and happens to be well off, her relationship with her American relatives is always utmost in her mind and of far more importance than money and social standing.

When Kate decides to live with her grandmother over other more exciting choices, she shows a nobility of character that Alcott thought she saw in the English people, who demonstrated great consider-

❧ ❧ ❧ ❧ ❧ ❧ ❧ ❧ ❧ ❧ ❧ ❧ ❧ ❧ ❧ ❧ ❧ ❧

ation for family and familial connections. Kate takes charge of bringing her new family together in much the same way that Alcott took charge of her own family and kept them together.

Gentle May Alcott took drawing lessons in Europe because sister Louisa paid for them and accompanied her on a European tour. When May married and later died while giving birth to a child, Louisa took over the raising of May's daughter Lulu. Louisa's mother, Abba, was able to retire from her job because Louisa paid the family bills and, no doubt, financed some of her father's philosophical projects. Certainly, Bronson Alcott had no money of his own.

Louisa and Kate were in some ways almost the same person: independent, domestic women determined to make a home.

What Love Can Do—

Louisa May Alcott was never able to entirely leave behind the effects of her childhood's poverty. Bronson Alcott was

🌾 🌾 🌾 🌾 🌾 🌾 🌾 🌾 🌾 🌿 🌾 🌾 🌾 🌾 🌾 🌾 🌾 🌾 🌾

such a spiritual man he once refused to work as a carpenter, though he was a good one, because to do so would have been to debase the purity of his soul. In fact Mr. Alcott barely approved of commerce at all.

Fortunately, the Alcotts had a beloved benefactor, who didn't mind working, named Ralph Waldo Emerson. Emerson contributed of his wealth to what the Alcotts called their "sinking fund." The funds were always sinking, it seemed. Emerson's generosity was so great that Louisa felt he literally kept their family from starving.

Thus, it is no surprise that the virtue of charity plays a large part in many of Alcott's stories. However difficult the struggle against poverty might be, kindness can make life bearable, even hopeful. In "What Love Can Do" the givers also receive a gift in that friendship dispels the isolation of a lonely set of boarders who instead are destined to grow in love and good feeling—and in humanity.

Gwen's Adventure in the Snow—

This story is not so much about charity as it is about courage. Gwen, the main character, is already charitable and even responsible to a great degree. She is almost a little mother to her tribe of boys and girls out for a winter frolic. Yet her leadership is tested when the entire group must retreat to their summerhouse when things go awry and they are stranded in a sudden storm. Once in the house, the boys and their adventures seem to take over and become the focus of the story. The little men even find provisions and cook the evening meal while Gwen must calm the nervous smaller children.

But "Gwen's Adventure in the Snow" is not necessarily stereotypical or intended to be. Unlike other feminine reformers of her day, Louisa May Alcott had a great fondness for boys. She found them sometimes spirited and energetic in ways that girls were not. Louisa, as something of a tomboy herself, wanted to see girls adopt a more outgoing attitude, and Gwen's adventure certainly left its mark on the young heroine.

For Louisa May Alcott, the storyteller, there is always a lesson to be learned from every unexpected development.

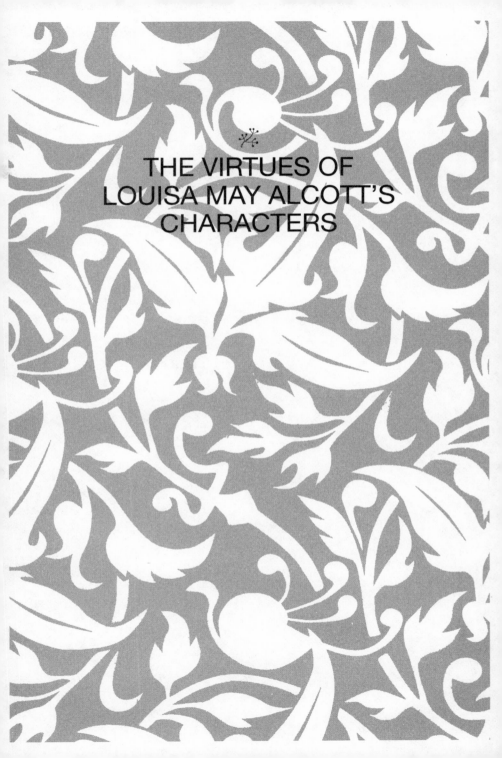

THE VIRTUES OF
LOUISA MAY ALCOTT'S
CHARACTERS

THE VIRTUES OF LOUISA MAY ALCOTT'S CHARACTERS

Louisa May Alcott was undoubtedly the most beloved children's author of her time, yet words such as "old maid" and "spinster" have been used to describe her. To some admirers who asked for a photograph, even she herself wrote: "You can't make a Venus out of a tired old lady."

How can such a self-deprecating woman have achieved such heights of literary fame and have accurately depicted the yearnings and aspirations of her youthful audience? Why did young readers sense in her such a friend and confidante when she had no children of her own? I believe we must look for our answers to these questions in the background of her family life.

Louisa May Alcott loved children and believed them capable of great moral maturity because she had parents who loved her and believed her capable of such attainments of character. The daughter of a schoolmaster father and a mother who was one of the first paid social workers in

✼ ✼ ✼ ✼ ✼ ✼ ✼ ✼ ✼ ✼ ✼ ✼ ✼ ✼ ✼ ✼ ✼ ✼ ✼

the United States, she had grown up in a household of high expectations.

Character and moral rectitude were everything in the Alcott household. The children were encouraged to speak about their feelings and aspirations, not with the purpose that these thoughts and feelings be indulged, but that they be molded and directed toward virtuous actions.

Father Bronson Alcott made it clear that he expected his little women to aspire to attributes of courage, loyalty, kindness, self-control, and sweet temper. Mother Abba Alcott made it clear that although she shared her husband's views on character development, she also understood that her children must be nurtured and allowed the freedom to have fun and be themselves—even if that meant they were less than little angels.

This may all seem like a tedious kind of goodness that reigned supreme in the Alcott home, but the Alcotts were not out of step with their times in these matters. Moral education was not something newly minted in America. Rather it had its origins in a Europe where French and German philosophers taught that goodness could be acquired through intuition and self-examination and that such pursuits were the whole goal of life.

In general, Louisa May Alcott felt blessed to have had such parents and responded well to such serious nurture. She developed a special love for her mother, who kept the family together when Father was out of work.

Out of this background, Louisa May's own aspirations became quite high. In a diary, she listed Love, Patience, Industry, and Generosity as among her life's goals. This diary was available to her parents, who regularly read it in order to encourage their daughter to aim high and believe in her perfectibility.

Is it any wonder that, though Louisa May Alcott's stories are entertaining, they are also earnest and instructive? This made her stories immensely popular with parents, and the children didn't seem to mind the dose of moral medicine that came with the stories, coming as it did from an "old maid" who loved boys and girls so well.

ABOUT
THE
AUTHOR

Louisa May Alcott is the beloved author of one of the world's great classics of literature, *Little Women.* First published in 1868, *Little Women* has captured the imaginations of countless generations of young adults who thrill to read the seemingly real-life adventures of Meg, Jo, Beth, and Amy of the impoverished March family.

A groundbreaking work at the time, Miss Alcott's story is one of the first books to treat children as real people, with real feelings and varied motives, in a realistic setting. Miss Alcott's characters hope, sorrow, and strive in a way that makes readers care for and believe in them.

With the success of *Little Women,* Louisa May Alcott became established as one of the leading lights of American literature and one of the most successful authors of her time. Although her fame was sudden, it did not come easily.

Born in 1832, Louisa May Alcott's fairy tale life did not have a fairy tale beginning. Her father, Bronson Alcott, was an earnest, impractical man who, without much formal education, decided to become a school-teacher and educational reformer. He failed in the educational profession several times, and with each failure came further poverty for his family. It was left to Louisa's mother, Abba Alcott, to give the family some semblance of emotional and financial stability.

Abba Alcott had to demonstrate a practicality that did not seem to dwell in the deep philosophical and educational recesses of Bronson Alcott's mind. Most assuredly the model for the character Marmee in *Little Women,* Abba became one of Boston's first social workers and, with her meager income, kept the family supplied as well as she could with material necessities.

Abba's example of self-sacrifice affected her daughter. From a very early age, Louisa May began to act the role of an adult and took it upon herself to do what she could to pull her family out of genteel, and sometimes not so genteel, poverty. She took any menial job to help out and was very aware of the fact that friend and neighbor Ralph Waldo Emerson had made them gifts of money over the years.

From very early on, Louisa Alcott was able to help the family by publishing short articles, poems, and stories in the various magazines that fed the voracious reading appetite of the Boston public. While these efforts never paid great sums of money, they did provide a little relief for the family and a lot of experience for Louisa.

Ironically enough, it was the Civil War that gave Miss Alcott her freedom to step out of the family shadows and into her own limelight.

In 1862, Louisa May Alcott volunteered to become a nurse in a Union hospital. The experience, though short, changed her life. After the briefest of training, she found herself caring for desperately ill and dying men. She discovered new strength in herself as she fed her charges, helped alleviate their sufferings, and ministered words of comfort to those who would not see home nor sweetheart again.

The work was exhausting, the conditions

for the nurses themselves appalling, and Louisa nearly died. Bronson Alcott had to go to Washington, D. C., to rescue her, and although she recovered rapidly, her health was never quite the same.

Out of this tragic experience came her war book, *Hospital Sketches.* In itself not a great success, the book did give evidence of a new maturity in Louisa's writing. This maturity was appreciated by her Boston publishers who became increasingly supportive of her work. Writing as much as thirty pages of copy a day, from this time forward, Miss Alcott never lacked an outlet for her writing.

Then, in 1868 came *Little Women,* instant fame, and the enormous sum of $8,000 in royalties. The family's financial worries were at an end. The very happy conclusion of *Little Women* really did mirror that of her own dear family except for one thing: Louisa May Alcott never married as Jo March did. That was a dream that was never to be.

Instead, Louisa May remained faithful to her family, nursing her mother through her last illness, and finally passing away herself in the same year her father died. From 1832 to 1888, it had been a short but eventful life.

ABOUT
THE
PRESENTER

About the Presenter

Stephen W. Hines is a writer, researcher, and editor who has worked with words on a professional basis for twenty years. His book, *Little House in the Ozarks: the Rediscovered Writings* (of Laura Ingalls Wilder), rose to the *Publishers Weekly* best-seller list in 1991. Since that time, he has devoted himself to the rediscovery of other worthy but overlooked efforts by famous authors.

Following several successful books on Laura Ingalls Wilder, Hines discovered *The Quiet Little Woman: A Christmas Story* by Louisa May Alcott in a long-forgotten children's magazine. This book appeared on the CBA best-selling hardcover fiction list for several months in 1999 and 2000.

Stephen lives with his wife and daughters near Nashville, Tennessee, where he continues his research and writes a column for a local paper. His books have sold more than one million copies.

⚘ ⚘ ⚘ ⚘ ⚘ ⚘ ⚘ ⚘ ⚘ ⚘ ⚘ ⚘ ⚘ ⚘ ⚘ ⚘ ⚘ ⚘

If you have enjoyed this book,
or if it has impacted your life,
we would like to hear from you.
Please contact us at:

RIVEROAK PUBLISHING
Department E
P.O. Box 700143
Tulsa, Oklahoma 74170-0143

Visit our website at:
www.riveroakpublishing.com